Published by
Bantam Doubleday Dell Books for Young Readers
a division of
Bantam Doubleday Dell Publishing Group, Inc.
1540 Broadway
New York, New York 10036

ISBN: 0-440-40829-6

Reprinted by arrangement with Doubleday Books
for Young Readers
Printed in the United States of America
September 1993
11 12 13 14 15 16 17 18 19 20 21 22 23

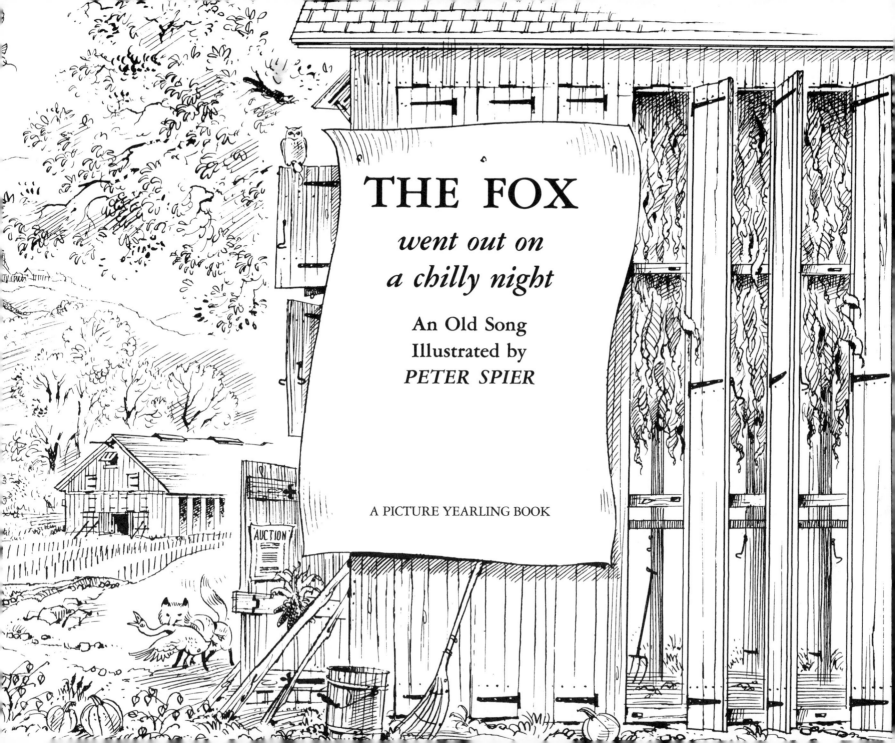

THE FOX

*went out on
a chilly night*

An Old Song
Illustrated by
PETER SPIER

A PICTURE YEARLING BOOK

The fox went out on a chilly night,

and he prayed to the moon to give him light,

for he'd many miles to go that night

before he reached the town-o, town-o, town-o,

for he'd many miles to go that night

before he reached the town-o.

He ran till he came to the farmer's bin,

where the ducks and the geese were kept penned in.

"A couple of you will grease my chin

before I leave this town-o, town-o, town-o.

A couple of you will grease my chin

before I leave this town-o."

First he caught the grey goose by the neck,

then he swung a duck across his back.

And he didn't mind the quack, quack, quack,

or their legs all dangling down-o, down-o, down-o.

And he didn't mind the quack, quack, quack,

or their legs all dangling down-o.

Then old mother Giggle-Gaggle jumped out of bed.

Out of the window she popped her head,

crying, "John! John! Our grey goose is gone,

and the fox is in the town-o, town-o, town-o,"

crying, "John! John! Our grey goose is gone

and the fox is in the town-o."

Then John, he ran to the top of the hill,

blew his horn both loud and shrill.

The fox, he said, "I better go with my kill

or they'll soon be on my tail-o, tail-o, tail-o."

The fox, he said, "I better go with my kill

or they'll soon be on my tail-o."

He ran till he came to his nice warm den.

There were the little ones, eight, nine, ten.

They said, "Daddy, better go back again,

because it must be a wonderful town-o, town-o, town-o."

Then the fox and his wife, without any strife,

cut up the goose with a fork and a knife.

They never ate such a dinner in their life

and the little ones chewed on the bones-o, bones-o, bones-o.

They never ate such a dinner in their life

and the little ones chewed on the bones-o.

2. He ran till he came to the farmer's bin,
   Where the ducks and the geese were kept penned in.
   "A couple of you will grease my chin
   Before I leave this town-o.
   A couple of you will grease my chin
   Before I leave this town-o."

5. Then John, he ran to the top of the hill,
   Blew his horn both loud and shrill;
   The fox, he said, "I better go with my kill
   Or they'll soon be on my tail-o."
   The fox, he said, "I better go with my kill
   Or they'll soon be on my tail-o."

3. First he caught the grey goose by the neck,
   Then he swung a duck across his back.
   And he didn't mind the quack, quack, quack,
   Or their legs all dangling down-o, down-o, down-o,
   And he didn't mind the quack, quack, quack,
   Or their legs all dangling down-o.

6. He ran till he came to his nice warm den,
   There were the little ones, eight, nine, ten.
   They said, "Daddy, better go back again,
   Because it must be a wonderful town-o, town-o, town-o."
   They said, "Daddy, better go back again,
   Because it must be a wonderful town-o."

4. Then old mother Giggle-Gaggle jumped out of bed,
   Out of the window she popped her head,
   Crying, "John! John! Our grey goose is gone
   And the fox is in the town-o, town-o, town-o,"
   Crying, "John! John! Our grey goose is gone
   And the fox is in the town-o!

7. Then the fox and his wife, without any strife,
   Cut up the goose with a fork and a knife;
   They never ate such a dinner in their life
   And the little ones chewed on the bones-o, bones-o, bones-o,
   They never ate such a dinner in their life
   And the little ones chewed on the bones-o.